For Liz Frink —MM

To my earliest inspirations:
Elisabeth Frink, Sue MacDougall, and my mother Roo —OLG

Text copyright © 2019 by Michael Morpurgo
Illustrations copyright © 2019 by Olivia Lomenech Gill

First US edition 2020
First published by Walker Books Ltd. (UK) 2019

Library of Congress Catalog Card Number pending
ISBN 978-1-5362-1288-4

20 21 22 23 24 25 APS 10 9 8 7 6 5 4 3 2 1

Printed in Humen, Dongguan, China

This book was typeset in Sabon.
The illustrations were done in mixed media.

Candlewick Press
99 Dover Street
Somerville, Massachusetts 02144

www.candlewick.com

CANDLEWICK PRESS

Muck & Magic

MICHAEL MORPURGO

illustrated by

OLIVIA LOMENECH GILL

UNTIL THAT MORNING, until my bike ride up into the Dales, I had always known exactly what I was going to do with my life. I was going to be the fastest woman ever on two wheels, a world champion cyclist, win an Olympic gold medal, and not just one. Three. I was going to be the next Laura Trott, no question.

I think I could ride a bike almost before I could walk. My mom had made sure of that. She loved cycling and spent every hour she could out on the road—when she wasn't being head teacher at the village school, that is. It was a new job for her, we were in a new house, and I was in a new school trying to make new friends, which wasn't easy. Dad stayed home and looked after us. He fed us, washed our clothes— no ironing, because he hated ironing—did the building of the racing bikes in his shed. The radio was always on inside, playing loud heavy metal, always heavy metal.

There were floor-to-ceiling photographs and newspaper cuttings in there of all our great cycling heroes and heroines. There was Beryl Burton, Mom's favorite, who had been a world champion a long while ago, before she or I were born. My hero, Laura Trott, was up there too, and so was Dad's: "Wiggo," Bradley Wiggins, or as Dad always called him, "The Wonderful Wiggo of Woz."

Dad didn't cycle anymore himself. He'd had a bad fall when he was young and broken his hip. Gruesomely, he kept a yellowing and grim reminder of his hip replacement operation right beside him on his workbench: his old hip joint. He would often rub it for luck and always made sure Mom and I did too before we went out for a ride. Neither of us had ever fallen off and hurt ourselves, not seriously anyway. Just a silly superstition, Mom called it. But she still gave it a lucky rub every time we went off for a ride, and so did I.

Like Mom I've always been rather short and thin, skinny some people say. All my life, Gran never stopped going on about it. "Our Bonny, just look at her," she'd say, measuring me up yet again against the kitchen door, a dreaded ritual whenever she came around for my birthday. "She don't grow upwards, nor sideways neither. There's hardly nothing of her." And it was true, I wasn't as tall as I wanted to be. Long legs are good for cycling and I longed for them. I desperately wanted to grow into a bigger bike, a faster one, a bike like Laura Trott's. At school I had always been "little Bonny." Now I was "tiddler" or "teeny

tot." Everyone ribbed me about my height. I didn't mind that much. After all, Laura Trott wasn't that tall, was she? And she was slight, well, quite slight. I could be small and still be a world champion, still win three Olympic gold medals. It could even help to be shorter, I thought. They could call me what they liked.

Of course everyone already knew at school and in the village that our whole family lived and breathed cycling.

They would see us out on the road, after school and on weekends, Mom and me pedaling away. Sometimes, when we were doing time trials, Dad would be there too with his stopwatch and whistle. We were quite a threesome, always out whatever the weather. Mom would never let a hill defeat her, and neither would I. The older I was, and the stronger I became, the more I found I could keep up with her.

That January, as we were cycling home together side by side, she told me that from now on perhaps I should go out on my own more often, that she felt she was holding me back. "And anyway," she went on, "I've got so much to do at school these days, and I'm not as young as I was. I'll still be your trainer though. You may be faster than me, Bonny, but you're not faster than my Beryl, nor your beloved Laura Trott, not yet."

So after that we would only go out cycling together occasionally, just for fun, on sunny weekends. Mostly I went out cycling on my own. I missed Mom being there, but I liked being on my own too. I could be Laura in my head much better with no one else around.

On the morning of the day that changed my life—my twelfth birthday it was—I realized as soon as I got up that Mom and Dad were much more excited than I was. I knew something was up. At breakfast they kept looking at each other knowingly and giggling like a couple of kids. Some private joke, I thought. Then without warning Dad was behind me and putting his hands over my eyes.

"Surprise, Bonny," he said. "No peeking." I heard Mom going out and coming back in again. Dad took away his hands. Mom was standing there with a brand-new racing bike. It was a red, all-aluminum, sixteen-speed Giordano Libero—a wonder bike! Maybe it wasn't like Laura's, a Pinarello Dogma F8 with a custom paint job, but it was a wonder bike all the same. I was speechless. Together, this bike and I would fly like the wind!

I don't remember finishing my breakfast. I was upstairs, into my cycling gear, downstairs, and out of the door in a flash. No goodbyes, just a wave and a thank-you, and I was gone. I didn't decide where to go. I just went. Within minutes I was up in the Dales, purring along on my beautiful, magnificent, supreme, wonderful new bike. Alone with the wind and the rain, I was in seventh heaven. I mooed at cows, cawed at crows, bleated at sheep. There were lambs sheltering under the stone walls, and the rain was turning to hail now, but I didn't mind. This was bliss. This was the best.

I was coming down the hill fast, I remember, too fast, but I still wanted to go faster. I looked up and saw some horses out in a field, gamboling about in the hail, tossing their heads and shaking their manes. It was those horses that distracted me—that's my excuse, anyway. A sheep came wandering out into the road in front of me, a lamb following her. I braked, and the wheels seemed to slide away from under me.

I found myself lying there on my back in the ditch, my head spinning. It was a while before I could sit up. A couple of sheep wandered past me up a farm track, as if nothing had happened. I could see at once that my knee was bleeding, but it didn't hurt. I got up. I could stand. I was wobbly, but I could stand. Hailstones were battering me, bouncing off my head. I stood the bike up and crouched down to examine it. Everything seemed fine—at first. Then I noticed that my front tire was flat, and not a little flat either, but completely deflated. My beautiful new bike was unscratched though, so far as I could see. I was relieved and annoyed at the same time and still trying to work out what to do next when

I became aware that I was being watched. Three horses were scrutinizing me from the other side of the stone wall: a massive bay hunter, a chubby-looking pony with a face like a chipmunk, and a tall gray horse with a fine-boned head. They were all looking at me over the wall. The little one nickered, then both the others did too. I never knew horses could laugh until then.

"Don't you laugh at me," I told them, and I wasn't just pretending to be mad either. "It was your fault I fell off.

And look at what you've done. Flat tire. Thank you very much. Now what am I supposed to do?"

Quite why I went over and patted them after that, I have no idea. I'd never been so close to horses before, but somehow I wasn't at all nervous of them. They seemed to want me to stay with them, to get to know me. They had kind eyes, all of them. They liked me. I reached out to stroke them. But it soon became evident, as they snuffled at my hand, that it was food they were after, a tidbit of some kind. I had none, but I patted and stroked them all, as equally as I could. That was important to them, I thought, because they seemed quite jealous of one another. I talked to them, told them who I was and all about Laura Trott. But after a while they became bored with me, or more likely fed up that I had no food to give them, and wandered off.

I watched them go, sad they were leaving me. Then a dog yapped and someone called from the farmhouse at the top of the track, and off they galloped, neighing and nickering away, their hooves thundering and throwing up

mud, their manes flowing. The sight of them racing up the field left me smiling inside.

I could see a woman in a headscarf and a long blue coat walking to the horses across the lawn below the farmhouse. She had a bucket in each hand and was shaking them and calling to the horses. She climbed the fence and emptied the buckets into a long trough, then stood back, the dog sitting at her heels, and watched them racing up the field toward her. That was when she looked up and noticed me. She stared at me for a few moments, then turned and walked away. She didn't even wave. Not very friendly, I thought. It was as she walked away that I noticed there were several animals on the lawn below the house, all standing very still. There was a buffalo, a wild boar, a baboon, and a horse lying down. And there were people too: a shepherd driving his sheep, a running man, again all absolutely still, as still as statues. It took me a while to realize that was exactly what they must be—statues.

By now I was cold and my leg ached. I had to get going. After a bit of a walk, a kind farmer gave me a lift back home to the village in his Land Rover, my bike in the back. It took a while—I had cycled much farther than I thought. At home, Mom tended to my knee and Dad to my bike. I told them how, where, and why the accident had happened, told them it was the horses' fault too—which made them smile. I mentioned the woman up at the farmhouse, who hadn't seemed at all friendly, and about the strange statues in her garden. Mom said she'd been up that way once or twice and remembered the statues, but had never seen anyone there.

My knee healed in time. Dad mended my puncture and checked that everything on my bike was as it should be— he wouldn't let me ride again until he'd finished. But I couldn't put those horses out of my mind. They galloped through my dreams, day and night. Once I was allowed to cycle again, I started planning all my training rides to go past that farm track at the bottom of the hill where I had fallen off, just so that I could see the horses again. I would see the lady in the scarf sometimes too, sitting outside on a step and sketching, or striding across the field in her long coat, the horses following her.

By now I'd given the horses names. The tall gray one I called Peg, after Pegasus, the legendary flying horse I had read about at school; the small one I always thought of now as Tiny Tim; and the great big bay became Big Ben to me. After a while, just riding by the horses wasn't good enough. I'd bring carrots for them, and I'd stop for a drink at the bottom of the hill, then wait by the stone wall for them to come for their tidbits. It wouldn't be long before I'd see them gallop down to the wall to greet me, whinnying and kicking up their hooves, and farting too sometimes, which made me smile. I loved feeding them, with their warm breath on my hand and their rubbery lips and whiskers.

15

fig i

fig ii

fig iii

fig iv

fig v

I'd make a fuss of them all, give each of them their carrots—more for Peg because she wasn't as pushy as the other two. I'd talk to her especially, whisper in her ear about my new school, and friends and enemies, about Mom and Dad and cycling. I loved every moment with my horses, but I always looked up from time to time at the farmhouse beyond, just in case I could catch sight of the lady in the long coat. The rare times I did, she would just lift her hand and walk away. I would wave back, because I wanted to be friendly, but she always kept her distance, never came over. I hoped to meet her and would always get back on my bike reluctantly. I would be back to homework after that—there was a lot of that now that I was in high school—and to the sameness of the house, Mom looking stressed after her day at school and Dad at work in his shed, heavy metal on full volume.

When I wasn't out cycling or doing my homework, I would lie in my room and find myself dreaming of those horses,

Peg in particular. I pictured myself riding her bareback through forests and meadows, up rutty mountain passes, and fording rushing streams where she'd stop to drink. I'd go to sleep at night under the stars lying down beside her, my head resting on her warm back. But when I woke, her back was always my pillow and I could hear Dad in the bathroom next door, gargling and spitting into the basin.

I lived for the moment when school was over and I could cycle off to feed the horses. Peg would rest her heavy head on my shoulder and I'd hear those carrots crunching inside her grinding jaw. As for my cycling ambitions, I still loved my bike and Laura Trott, still wanted to be Olympic champion three times over; but I knew I went for cycle rides now not just to train and to go faster, not only to leave home and school behind me, but even more to see my horses, and maybe one day to meet the lady in the scarf and the long blue coat.

It was spring. Mom was threatening to come out on training rides with me again. I think she had picked up on my lack of focus, that I might have other things on my mind besides cycling. Dad knew it too. "She's got to learn to motivate herself," I heard him telling her. "You can't do it for her. We have to leave her be." So for the most part I could still go out on my own, to my great relief, and when I did it was always in the same direction, up into the Dales, to my horses.

It was a bright, cold Saturday morning and I was off and out early on my bike. The roads were dry, so I rode fast. I got to the end of the farm track in twenty-five minutes—a record. There were daffodils growing now all along the grass verge by the stone wall, so many it was hard to find a way through without treading on them. I leaned my bike up against the wall as usual and fished in my pocket for the carrots. Tiny Tim came scampering over as he always did, and Big Ben wandered lazily up behind him, his tail flicking nonchalantly. But there was no sign of Peg in the field at all. When Big Ben had finished his carrot, he started chewing at the saddle of my bike and knocked it over. I was just picking it up when I saw the lady in the long coat striding down the field toward me, her little dog yapping at her heels. She wasn't wearing her usual headscarf. I saw that her hair was entirely white, a wild curly mop, almost down to her shoulders. Her face was somehow both old and young at the same time.

"Who are you?" she asked. It was just a straight question, not a challenge.

"Bonny," I replied.

"I've seen you here before, haven't I?" she asked me. "You like the horses?"

I nodded. "Especially the gray one. But she's not here today."

"It's the spring grass. I have to keep her inside from now on."

"Why?" I asked. The dog was snuffling around my feet. I stood still, hoping it wasn't the biting kind.

"Percy won't hurt you. All bark and no bite," she said. "Laminitis," she went on. "She gets it easily on new grass. She's fine all through the winter, eats all the grass she likes, no trouble. But she's only got to sniff the spring grass and the laminitis comes back. It heats the hoof, makes her lame." She waved away the two horses. She was scrutinizing me and my bike. "Nice bike. Fast, is it?"

I smiled. "Very," I said.

"So are the horses, some of them—not that little fellow of course. But they're an awful lot of work."

"Work?" I didn't understand.

"Well, Bonny, you have to bring them in, groom them, pick out their feet, feed them, muck them out. Heavy work. And I'm not as young as I was." She paused, looking at me hard for a moment or two. "You don't want a job, do you, in the stables? Be a big help. Merry, the one with laminitis, needs a good long walk every day, and all of them a good

23

mucking out. Paying job of course. Three pounds an hour, what do you say?"

"Yes," I said. I didn't have to think about it.

"You could come for a couple of hours on the weekends," she went on. "How would that be?"

"Fine," I said.

"I'll see you next Saturday then, Bonny," she said. "You'll need wellies. I've got some spare ones somewhere, for my nephew when he comes. You're about his size I should think. I'll look for them. You be careful on the roads now. Don't go too fast. You don't want to fall off, do you? Lot safer on a horse." She smiled at me then, in a knowing sort of way. She must have seen me come off that day. She turned and walked away.

I cycled home that day singing my heart out and high as a kite. It was my first paying job, and I'd be looking after Peg—it was difficult to think of her as Merry. I didn't tell anyone at home. So far as they were concerned, I

was out training on my bike. They were always happy if I was doing that. Where I went on my bike was my own business. Best just to keep everything to myself, I thought, less complicated. So next Saturday I found myself cycling up the farm track toward the house. It was full of potholes and puddles. I had to go carefully so that I didn't damage my bike. I came out onto a smooth tarmac lane, under an avenue of high trees that whispered at me in the wind as I cycled by, where I could pedal freely and hear the comforting *tic-a-tac tic-a-tac* of my wheels turning.

Everywhere in among the trees were more creatures: deer, foxes, badgers, all still, all looking at me, all statues. And there, by the house, were the sculptures I had seen before, the life-size buffalo, baboon, wild boar, and lying-down horse and the running man, a giant now that I was close to him, along with the shepherd and his sheep.

There was a cobbled stable yard behind the house. Peg was looking out at me over the stable door, ears pricked, shaking her mane, tossing her head and whinnying. Above the yard a flock of doves fluttered around a clock tower and then settled on the tiled roof, cooing at me. I didn't like to call out to the lady. I went over to Peg, gave her a carrot, and stroked her nose. "Morning, Peg," I said. "S'pose I'd better call you Merry. Morning, Merry." That was when I noticed a pair of wellies waiting by the back door of the house, with a piece of paper slipped into one of them. I took it out and read:

HOPE THE BOOTS FIT.
TAKE MERRY FOR A WALK DOWN THE
TRACKS, NOT IN THE FIELDS. SHE CAN NIBBLE
THE GRASS BUT NOT TOO MUCH. THEN MUCK
OUT THE STABLES. SAVE WHAT DRY STRAW
YOU CAN — IT'S EXPENSIVE!
WHEN YOU'VE DONE, SHAKE OUT HALF

A BALE IN HER STABLE – YOU'LL FIND STRAW AND HAY IN THE BARN. SHE HAS TWO SLICES OF HAY IN HER RACK. DON'T FORGET TO FILL UP THE WATER BUCKETS, AND BOLT THE STABLE DOOR WHEN YOU LEAVE – VERY IMPORTANT!

It was not signed.

Until then I had not given it a single thought, but I had never led a horse or ridden one in all my life. Come to think of it, I hadn't mucked out a stable either. Merry had a halter on her already, and a rope hung from a hook beside the stable. I put the wellies on—they were only a little too big—clipped the rope onto the halter, opened the stable door, and led her out, praying she would behave. I needn't have worried. It was Merry that took me for a walk. I simply stopped whenever she did, let her nibble for a while, and then asked her gently if it wasn't time to move on.

29

She knew the way—up the track through the woods, past more running men and another wild boar, then forking off past a pond where a huge bronze water buffalo stood in the water, drinking without ever moving his lips. White fish glided in a ghostly fashion through the dark of the water under the shadow of his nose. The path led upward from there and took us past a henhouse where some speckled black and white hens scuttled about, and a solitary goose stretched his neck, flapped his wings, and honked at us. Merry stopped for a moment, lifted her nose, and wrinkled it at the goose, who began preening himself busily. After a while I found myself coming back to the stable-yard gate, Merry leading me in. I tied her up in the yard and set about mucking out the stables.

So it went on, every Saturday morning for a month or more. The lady was never there, so I had the place to myself. She always left me a note of instructions in my wellies. Then, one Saturday I was emptying the wheelbarrow onto the muckheap when I felt someone behind me. I turned around.

Without her coat she looked a lot thinner than I had imagined, and more frail. She was dressed in jeans and a rough sweater, and her face and hands seemed to be covered in white powder, as if someone had thrown flour at her.

"Where there's muck there's money, that's what they say," she said with a laugh. "Not true, I'm afraid, Bonny. Where there's muck, there's magic. Now that *is* true." I wasn't sure what she meant by that. "Horse muck," she went on, by way of explanation. "Best magic in the world for vegetables. I've got leeks in my garden longer than, longer than . . ." She looked around her. "Twice as long as your bicycle pump over there. All the soil asks is that we feed it with that stuff, and it'll do whatever we want it to. It's like anything, Bonny—you have to put more in than you take out. You want some tea when you've finished?"

"Yes, please."

"Come up along into the house when you're done then. You can have your money. Haven't paid you yet at all, have I? And you've done a lot of Saturdays." She laughed at that.

"Maybe there is money in muck after all."

As I watched her walk away, Percy came bustling across the lawn toward her and sprang up into her arms. She lifted him onto her shoulder, where he balanced easily and rode her into the house.

I finished mucking out the stable as quickly as I could, shook out some fresh straw, filled up the water buckets, and led Merry back in. I gave her a goodbye pat on the neck and another carrot and left her to her hay. "Bye, Peg," I said. When I talked to her I still thought of her as Peg.

I found the lady in the kitchen, cutting bread. Percy yapped at me from his basket until she told him to be quiet.

"I've got peanut butter or honey," she said. I didn't like either, but I didn't say so.

"Honey, please," I replied. She carried the mugs of tea and I carried the plate of sandwiches. I followed her out across a cobbled courtyard, accompanied by Percy, down some steps and into a great glass building where there stood a life-size sculpture of a great white horse. "You recognize her?" she asked me. "You couldn't mistake her."

"It's Peg, isn't it?" I said in amazement. "She was always Peg to me before I knew she was Merry," I explained.

"Peg, Merry, she won't mind," she laughed. "I don't think I told you my name, did I, Bonny? That was rude of me. I'm Liz Maloney. You can call me Lizzie. I prefer it."

The floor was covered in newspaper, and everywhere was crunchy underfoot with plaster. The shelves all around were full of heads, arms, legs, and hands. A white sculpture of a dog stood guard over the plate of sandwiches and never even sniffed them. Lizzie sipped her tea between her hands and looked up at the giant horse. The horse looked just like Merry, only a lot bigger.

"It's no good," she said, standing back and walking around the horse, scrutinizing her from all sides. "She needs a good rider." She turned to me suddenly. "You wouldn't be the rider for me, would you, Bonny? You could be just who I need. Could you ride Merry for me?"

"I can't ride."

35

WOODEN MALLET

COLD CHISEL

WOOD CHISEL

OUTSIDE CALIPERS

PLIERS

TIN SNIPS

PINCERS

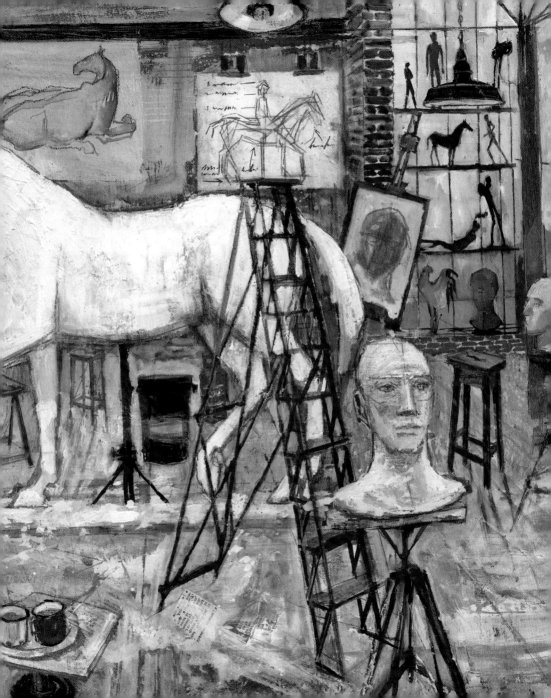

"You can ride a bike, can't you? It's not that different. And anyway, you wouldn't have to, not really. You'd just sit there on Merry and I'd sketch you, sculpt you."

"What, now?" I asked.

"Next week. Next Saturday. That be all right?" she said.

So it was that the next Saturday I found myself sitting astride Merry-Peg in the stable yard—we decided between us to call her both names from then on. She was pulling contentedly at her hay net and paying no attention to us whatsoever. It felt strange up there—so much higher off the ground than on a bike, with Merry-Peg shifting, warm underneath me. There was no saddle. Lizzie told me to hold the reins one-handed, loosely, to "sit easy," and "feel part of the horse." The worst of it was that I was hot, stifling hot, because I was in desert dress. I had great swathes of cloth over and around my head and

draped down to my feet with a long heavy robe so that nothing could be seen of my jeans or sweater or wellies.

"When you come next week, you can give me a hand making you—if you see what I'm saying! I'm not as strong as I was, and I'm in a hurry to get on with this and to make the rider, make you. You can mix the plaster for me. Would you like that?" Merry-Peg snorted and pawed the ground. "I'll take that as a yes, shall I?" she said, laughing, and walked around behind the horse, turning over the page of her sketch pad. "I want to do one more from this side and one from the front, then you can go home."

Half an hour later when she let me down and unwrapped me, my legs had pins and needles, and my bottom felt stiff as a board.

"Can I see the sketch?"
I asked her.

"I'll show you next week,"
she said. "You will come,
won't you?"

She knew I would, and I did. Because it was spring break, I came every day after that to muck out the stables and to walk Merry-Peg as usual, but what I looked forward to most—even more than being with Merry-Peg—was mixing up Lizzie's plaster for her in the bucket, climbing the stepladder with it, holding it for her, and watching her lay the strips of cloth dunked in the wet plaster over the frame of the rider—who she always referred to as Bonny. I liked that. She was building me up slowly, strip by strip, from the skeleton of the wire frame, into what looked at first like an Egyptian mummy.

After only a few days' work, I had become a rider looking out over the desert, at one with my horse, my robes shrouding me with mystery. It was me inside that skeleton, me inside that mummy-looking creature. Lizzie worked ceaselessly, and with such a fierce determination that I didn't like to interrupt. We were joined in a common but comfortable silence.

At the end of a month or so we stood back, the two of us, and looked up at the finished horse and rider.

"Well," said Lizzie, her hands on her hips. "What do you think, Bonny?"

"I wish," I whispered, reaching up and touching the neck of the horse, "I just wish I could do it, make such a thing, make a sculpture."

"But you did, Bonny," she said, and I felt her hand on my shoulder. "We did it together. I couldn't have done it without you." She was a little breathless when she spoke. "Without you, that horse would never have had a rider. If you weren't here, I don't think I would ever have even thought of giving her a rider. And she needed one. Without you mixing my plaster, holding the bucket, I couldn't have done it." Her fingers gripped my shoulder tighter. "Do you want to make a sculpture of your own, Bonny?"

"I can't."

"Of course you can. But you have to look around you first, not just glance, but really look. You have to breathe the world in deep, and all its creatures too, become a part of it. You draw what you see, what you feel, what you know, what you care about. After that, you make what you've drawn. Use clay if you like, or do what I do and build plaster over a wire frame. Then set to work with your chisel, just like I do, until it's how you want it. If I can do it, you can do it. I tell you what. You can have a corner of my studio if you like, just so long as you don't talk when I'm working. How's that?"

As spring blossomed into summer, I was away on my bike as often as possible. I couldn't avoid Mom riding out with me sometimes, or Dad being there occasionally with his stopwatch for time trials. He said he thought I'd reached a plateau of performance, that it happens and I wasn't to worry about it, but that my times weren't improving as much as he hoped, which surprised him, he said, with all the training I had been doing. I was leading a kind of double life, and I was loving every moment of it.

I could even ride now. After a while, I dared to ride Merry-Peg bareback on the way back to her stable, and I never forgot what Lizzie had told me. I looked about me. I listened. I breathed the world in deep. And the more I listened and looked, the more I felt at home in this new world. I became a creature of the place. I belonged there as much as the wren that sang at me from up high on the vegetable garden wall, as much as the green dragonfly hovering over the pool by the water buffalo. I sketched Merry-Peg. I sketched Big Ben. I couldn't sketch Tiny Tim, because he wouldn't ever stand still, and he just came out round. I bent my first wire frame into shape and I began to build a small horse sculpture, layer on layer of strips of cloth dunked in plaster. I molded them into shape around the frame, and when they dried I chipped away and sanded. But I was never happy with what I'd done.

All this time, Lizzie was working away beside me in the studio, harder, faster, more intensely than ever. I helped her whenever she asked me to, mixing and holding the bucket for her, just as I had done before.

The silences between us were always comfortable. We were in a world of our own. I didn't ask questions about her new sculpture, though I was aching to. I'd learned to wait for her to tell me. "It's going to be a figure of a walking woman," she said. "They want me to make a sculpture for the church. They told me I can do what I like. So I am. I like doing what I like. *Striding Woman*, I am calling her." From time to time she'd come over and look at my stumpy effort that looked as much like a dog as a horse to me, and she would walk around it nodding her approval. "Coming on, coming on," she'd say. "Maybe just a little bit off here perhaps." And she'd chisel away for a minute or two, and a neck or leg would suddenly come to life.

"When you do it, it's like magic," I told her. She thought for a moment and said, "No, Bonny. Not magic. It's a given thing, a gift from who knows where, who knows who, but once you discover you have it, whatever the gift is, it's not to be wasted. You have to learn to believe in it, work on it. Don't waste it, Bonny. Don't ever waste it. Life's too short to waste it."

The horse and rider came back from the foundry, bronze now and magnificent. I marveled at it. It stood outside her studio, and when it caught the red of the evening sun, I could scarcely take my eyes off it. But these days, I noticed, Lizzie seemed to be tiring more easily, and she would sit longer over her tea, gazing out at her sculpture and lapsing into long silences.

"I am so pleased with our horse and rider," she told me, "so pleased we did it together."

The *Striding Woman* figure was finished by then and went off to the foundry a few weeks before I was going on my summer holiday. "By the time you come back," said Lizzie, "it should be all done and back from the foundry. It's going to stand outside the church door in the village so that everyone can take her by the hand if they like—that's why she's holding it out. We all need a helping hand from time to time, don't we, Bonny?"

Our holiday that summer was in Cornwall as usual. We stayed where we always did, in St. Ives, and I drew every day. I drew boats and gulls, lobster pots and fishermen. I made sculptures with wet sand—sleeping giants, turtles, whales—and I swam a lot too. Mom and Dad seemed surprised and puzzled at my new passion for drawing, but were delighted, I could tell, when my sand sculptures attracted enthusiastic crowds each day. The sun shone for fourteen days. I never had such a perfect holiday. But I missed the horses, and Lizzie, and was looking forward to showing her my sketches.

The first day home, I cycled out to see her with a few of my best drawings in a stiff envelope in my backpack. As I came up the farm track, the place looked strangely still. The stable yard was deserted. There were no horses in the fields. Merry-Peg wasn't in her stable, no wellies by the door. I knocked on the door, rang the bell, called for her. Everything was quiet around the house, no Lizzie, no yapping Percy. I cycled to the nearest village and tried to find someone to ask. It was like a ghost village. Then I heard the church bell ringing. I leaned my bike up against the churchyard wall and went up the path. Just as she had said it would be, Lizzie's *Striding Woman* stood there glowing in the sun beside the church porch. Inside they were singing hymns.

I crept in, lifting the latch carefully so that I wouldn't be noticed. The hymn was just finishing. Everyone was sitting down and coughing. I found a place to sit right at the back behind the font. The church was packed. A choir in red robes and white surplices sat on either side of the altar. The vicar was up in the pulpit now, taking off her glasses. I looked everywhere for Lizzie's wild white curls, but couldn't find her. A few of the ladies were wearing hats, so I presumed she was too and stopped looking for her. She'd be there somewhere.

The vicar was speaking: "Last Saturday, a week ago now, Lizzie came here to unveil her beautiful *Striding Woman* sculpture. We were all here celebrating her gift to the church, to the parish, to all of us who live here. Sadly, so sadly, she died at home that same evening. Some will think of this powerful statue as a Madonna, some as a figure of womankind, but to me she will always be Lizzie. I think many of you will think the same."

It was at that moment that I caught sight of the coffin

resting on trestles between the choir stalls, a single wreath of white flowers laid on it. Only then did I begin to take in the awful truth.

I didn't cry when they carried the coffin out of the church, coming right by me. I suppose I was still trying to believe it. I stood and listened to the last prayers over the grave, numb inside, grieving as I had never grieved before or since, but still not crying. I waited until almost everyone had gone and went over to the grave. I didn't want to look down at the coffin. A man was taking off his jacket and hanging it on the branch of the tree. He spat on his hands, rubbed them, and picked up his spade. He saw me standing there.

"You family?" he said.

"Sort of," I replied. I reached inside my backpack and pulled out my best boat drawing from St. Ives. "Can you put it with her?" I asked. "It's a drawing. It's for Lizzie."

"'Course," he said, and he took the drawing from me

and looked down at it. "Nice, she'd like that. Fine lady, she was. The things she made. She saw everything beautiful, made everything beautiful. Magic, pure magic."

It was just before Christmas that same year that a cardboard tube arrived in the post, addressed to me. I opened it in the secrecy of my room. A rolled letter fell out, typed and very short.

Dear Bonny Marshall,

In her will, the late Lizzie Maloney instructed us, as her solicitors, to send you this drawing. We would ask you to keep us informed of any future changes of address.

With best wishes,

Benedict Lane

Solicitor

I unrolled it and spread it out. It was of me sitting on Merry-Peg, swathed in desert clothes. Underneath was written:

Dearest Bonny,

In the end, I don't think I paid you properly for all that mucking out and modeling, did I? And you never once asked. You shall have this instead, and when you are twenty-one, you shall have the artists' copy of the bronze of our Horse & Rider sculpture.

But by then, maybe you will be doing your own sculptures, if that is what you wish to do.

God Bless,
Lizzie

So here I am, well over thirty now, twenty years on. And as I look out at the settling snow from my studio window, I see Lizzie's *Horse and Rider* under the oak tree in my back garden, and all around my own sculptures are gathered. There are several hares, a prowling panther, a standing bear, and some sculptures of people too, one of Mom and Dad sitting together—they did get used to not having the next Laura Trott for a daughter in time—and one of the great Laura herself, standing proudly beside her bike. You try sculpting a racing bike. Not easy. I sent the drawing of it to her. She wrote a kind letter back, saying she wished she could draw like that. And I thought: sculpting, bike racing—we all do our own thing as best we can. The important thing is to love doing it.